For my very own Boy, with love

Copyright © 2004 by James Mayhew

First published in the United Kingdom in 2004 by The Chicken House, 2 Palmer Street, Frome, Somerset, BA 11 1DS. Email: *chickenhouse@doublecluck.com*

All rights reserved. Published by Scholastic Inc., *Publishers since 1920*, by arrangement with The Chicken House.
SCHOLASTIC and associated logos are trademarks and/or registered trademarks of Scholastic Inc. THE CHICKEN HOUSE is a registered trademark of Chicken House Publishing Limited.

Designed by Ian Butterworth and Elizabeth B. Parisi

Library of Congress Cataloging-in-Publication data available

ISBN 0-439-65106-9

10 9 8 7 6 5 4 3 2 1   04 05 06 07 08

Printed and bound in Singapore

First American edition, October 2004

BOY

James Mayhew

The Chicken House
Scholastic Inc.
New York

Boy woke up.
It was cold in the cave.
"Where's warm?" asked Boy.
"Here with us," said Ma and Pa.
"There's no room for me,"
said Boy. "Let me take your place."
"You'll have to share," said Ma and Pa.
But Boy didn't want to.

Boy went outside and waited for the sun to come up.
"Soon it will be warm," he thought.
But it was a cloudy day.
Boy felt colder than ever.

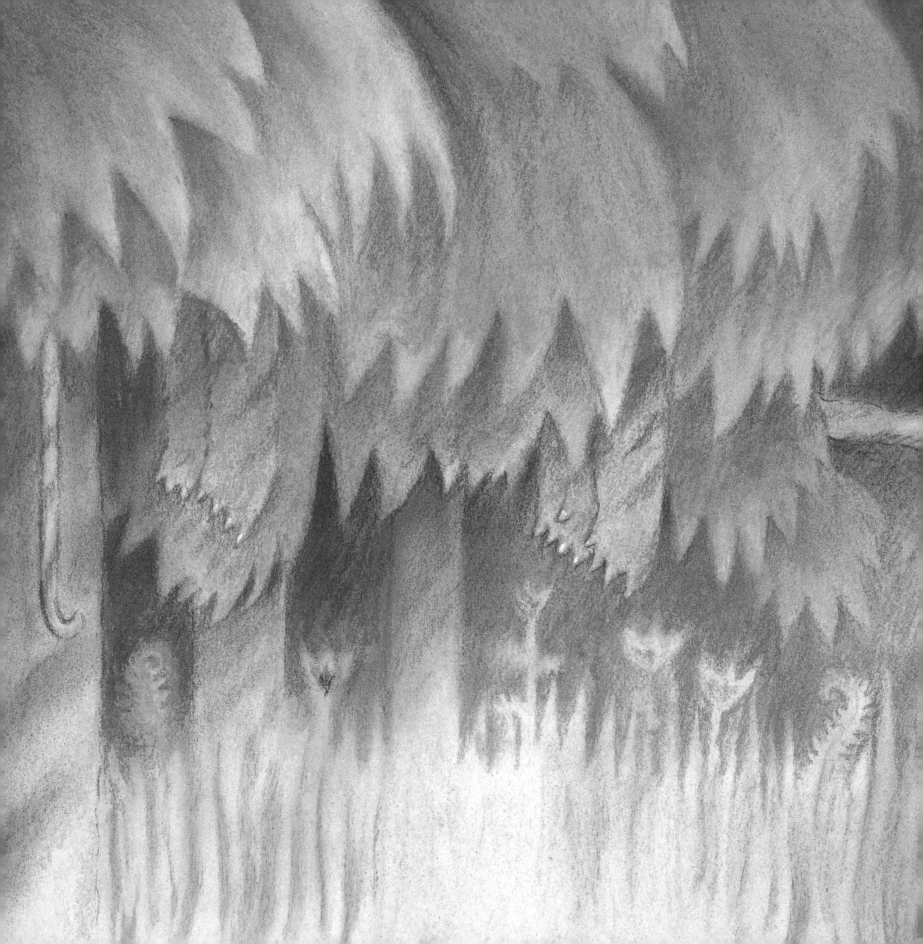

Boy walked through the leafy green
forest and sat in a tree.
"Here's warm," he thought.

"GRRRRRRR!" growled a hungry saber-toothed tiger. "This is my place. You can't stay here." "Why not?" asked Boy. "Because I might eat you up!" said the saber-toothed tiger.

Boy didn't like that idea at all,
so he ran off and sat in the tall yellow grass.
"Here's warm," he thought.

"Tarooooooot!"
roared
a woolly mammoth.
"This is my place.
You can't stay here!"
"Why not?" asked Boy.
"Because I might step on you,"
said the woolly mammoth.

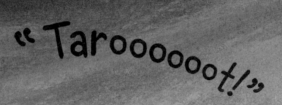

Boy didn't like that idea at all,
so he ran off and sat down on
a round red rock.
"Here's warm," he thought.

Boy didn't like that idea, either,
so he ran over the hill and up a mountain.
"Here's warm," he thought. "Here's very warm."
And he lay down in the sand and fell asleep.

KA-BOOOOM!

The ground began to shake and
the sky was filled with smoke.
Suddenly, it was too warm for Boy.
It was a fiery volcano!

Boy ran back over the round red rocks . . .

back through the tall yellow grass . . .

back through the leafy green forest . . .

. . . and back into the cold dark cave.

He climbed under the
blanket with Ma and Pa.
"Here's warm," thought Boy.
"Can I share with you?" he asked.
"Yes," said Ma and Pa.

And there was just enough room.